Star Stuff

By

Jenna Garzaniti

Illustrated by
Edith Schmidt

We're made of star stuff. We are a way for the cosmos to know itself".
-Carl Sagan

Dedicated to Sam, my forever stardust.

Jenna Garzaniti

To the Star Stuff that draws us all together

Edith Schmidt

Billions of light years agao there was a magnificent star.

It shone brighter than any star in its galaxy, it shone as bright as any star can shine in the universe

It could be seen as the brightest star by almost every planet within its view.

It was a guiding star, a beacon for the lost, a comfort for the found.

ITS WARMTH AND NOURISHING RAYS CREATED UNIQUE AND WONDEROUS LIFE

ON ALL THE PLANETS WITHIN ITS SOLAR SYSTEM.

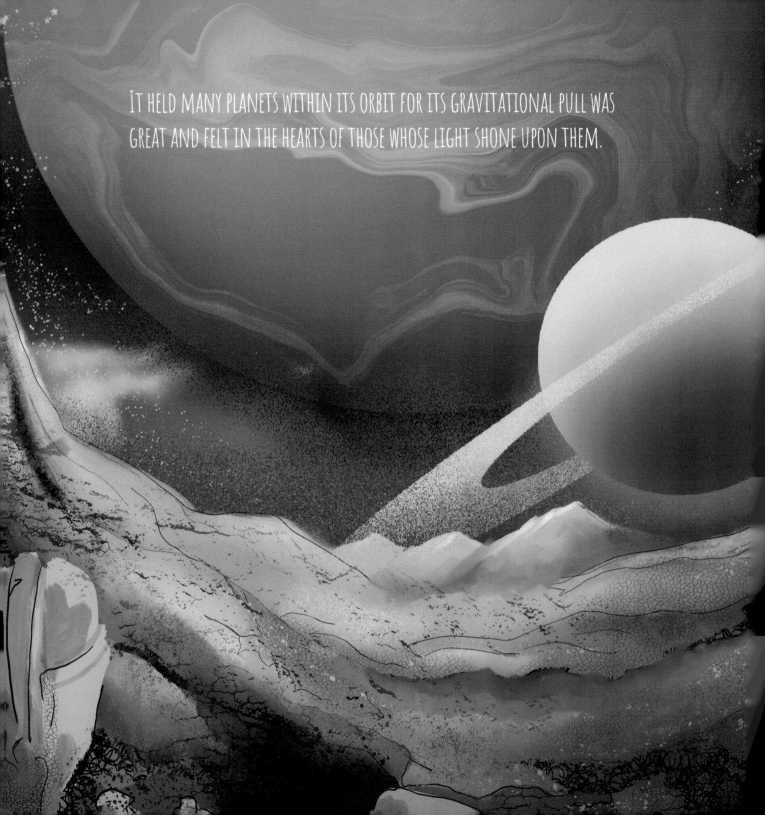

It held many planets within its orbit for its gravitational pull was great and felt in the hearts of those whose light shone upon them.

The star was worshiped. The star was loved, and lived a long, bright, dazzling life, until...

EVEN THE BRIGHTEST STAR BURNS OUT ONE DAY. EVERY PARTICLE, EVERY ATOM AND MOLECULE OF THE GREAT STAR SCATTERED THROUGH ITS GALAXY AND INTO OUR KNOWN UNIVERSE.

CENTURY AFTER CENTURY AFTER MILLENNIA EVERY LAST BIT OF THE STAR BECAME PART OF EACH WORLD

In every particle remained the memory of what it once was.

EVERY PARTICLE, EVERY ATOM, EVERY MOLECULE OF THE GREAT STAR
MISSED SHINING SO BRIGHTLY TOGETHER.

A BILLION LIGHT YEARS LATER YOU AND I WERE MADE. NOTHING COMES
FROM NOTHING OUR ATOMS ARE OF EARTH,

AND OUR EARTH IS MADE OF THE UNIVERSE AND STARS.

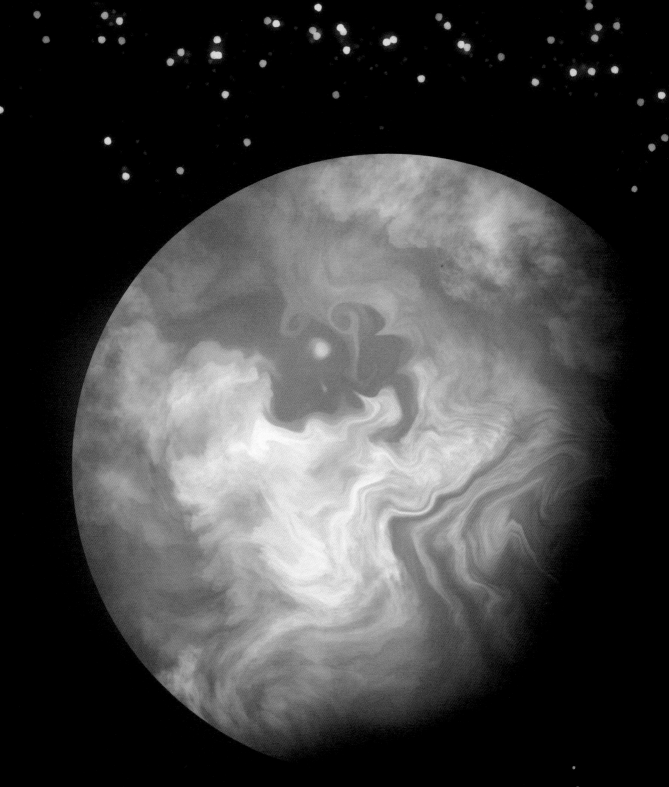

AND INSIDE OF YOU THERE IS ONE ATOM OF THE GREAT STAR.

AND INSIDE OF ME THERE IS ONE ATOM OF THE GREAT STAR.

And when the atom in you and the atom in me found each other, we found each other.

We found that together we SHINE

The gravity of our Great Star particles pulls us together so strongly that being apart creates an ache inside us.
When we are together, we are once again part of the Great Star, we are home.

"FOR SMALL CREATURES SUCH AS WE THE VASTNESS IS BEARABLE ONLY THROUGH LOVE"
-CARL SAGAN